Why can't I see in the dark?

Written by Anna Cowper
Illustrated by Ángeles Peinador

Collins

What's in this book?
Listen and say

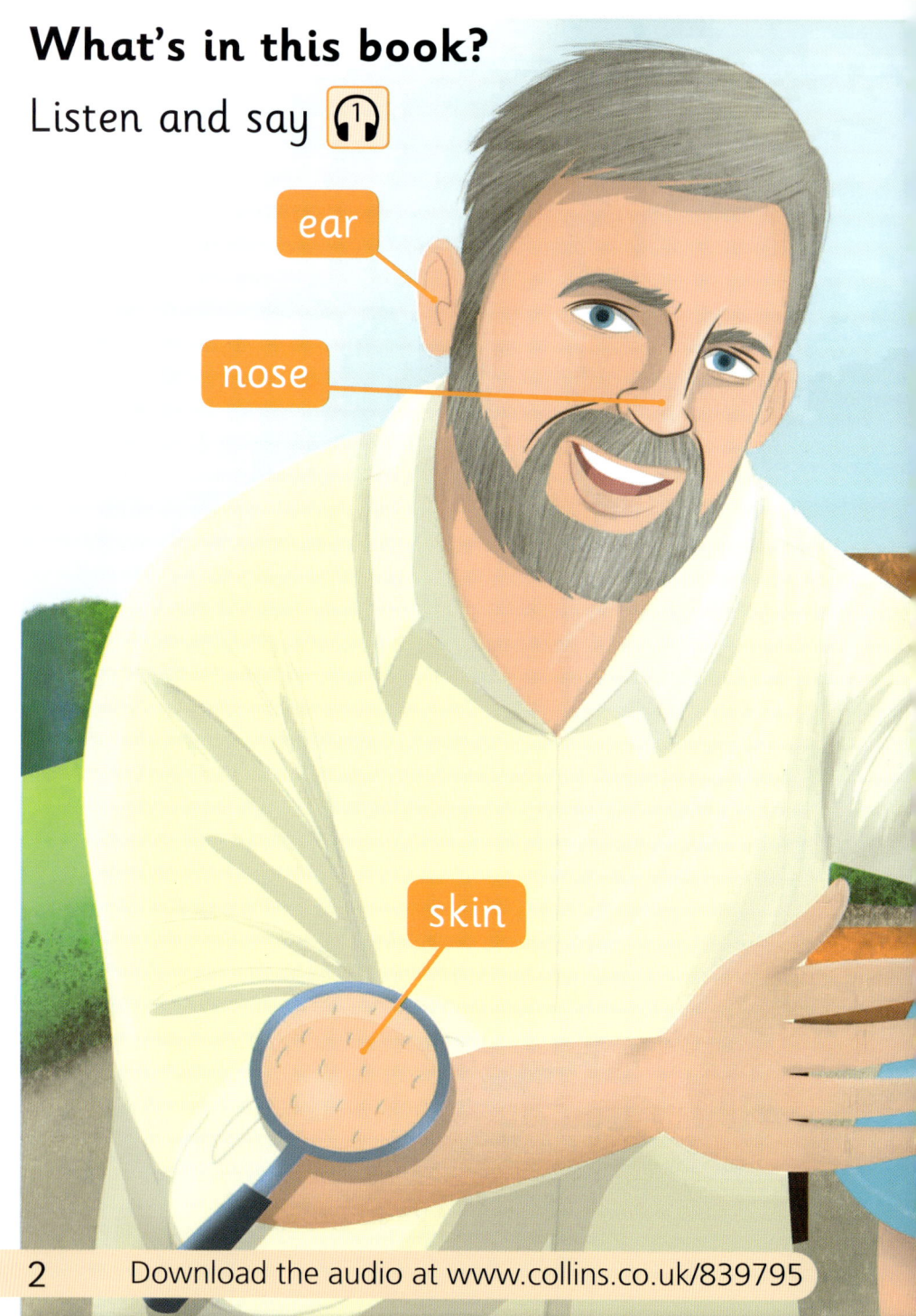

My grandad and me

Before reading

Grandad said, "Listen. It's an owl."
Stan asked, "What's an owl?"
Grandad said, "It's a bird. It flies at night."
Stan asked, "How can a bird fly at night? You can't see at night."

Grandad said, "Owls can see in the dark."
Stan said, "Why can't I see in the dark?"

Our eyes need light to see. In the day, we get light from the sun.

Look! The light goes on to the bird. Then, the light comes from the bird to your eye. Your eyes make a picture of the bird.

Grandad said, "Look. It's the owl. Can you hear the sound it makes?"

Stan said, "Yes! *Hoot hoot!* Grandad, do we need light to hear?"

No, we don't need light to hear. We hear with our ears. We hear sound.

Sound moves in the shape of a wave. The *sound waves* go into your ears and hit your eardrum.

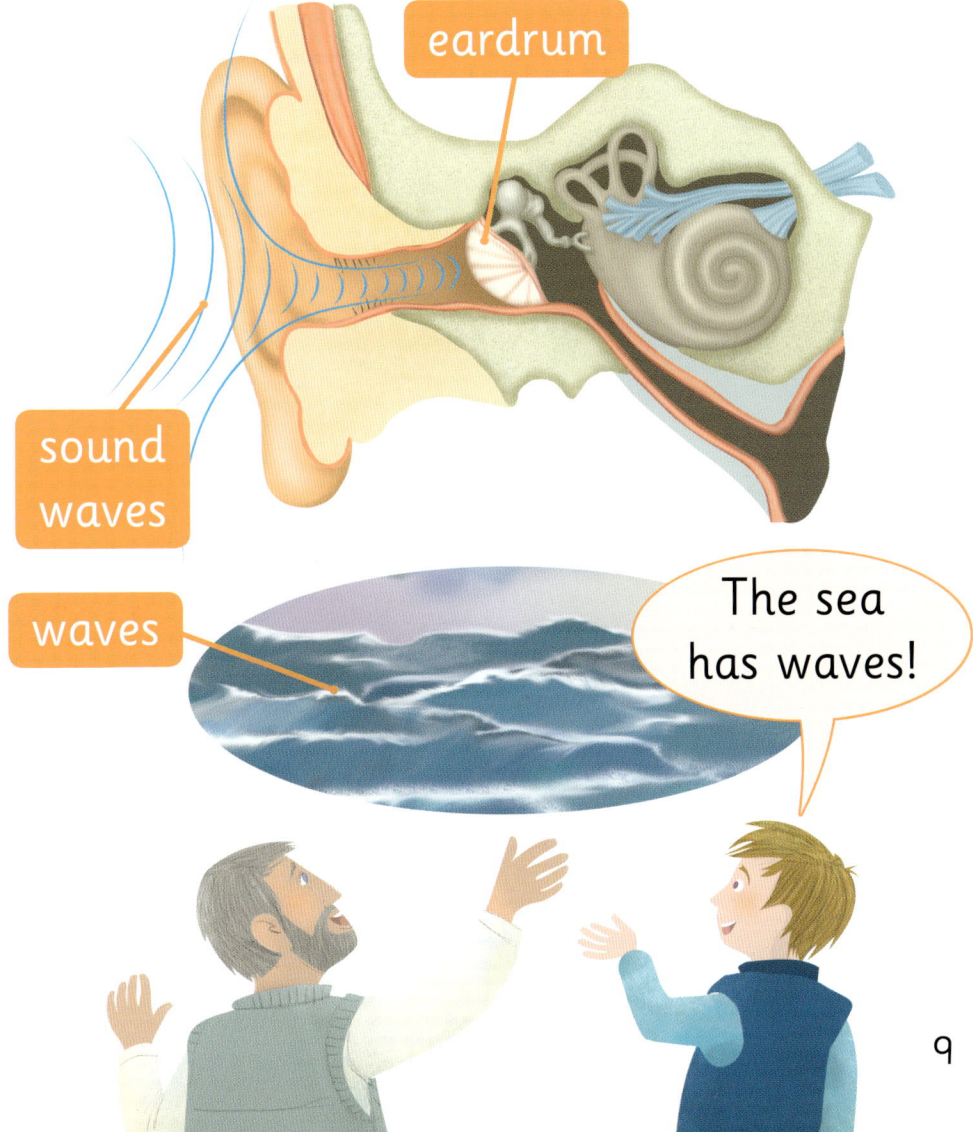

There are beautiful sounds:
music,
birds singing,
the sound of the sea.
And there is NOISE!
lots of cars and buses and motorbikes,
people shouting,
noisy machines.
Noise can make our ears hurt!

ear protectors

Loud noises can be bad for our ears.
It's a good idea to wear ear protectors.
These make our ears safe.

Stan asked, "What can I smell?"

Grandad said, "The flowers. They smell nice."

Stan asked, "Does *smell* move in waves?"

A smell is lots of very small things we can't see. They are *molecules*.

The molecules go into your nose. The hairs in your nose know what smell it is.

There are lots of good smells:
red strawberries,
hot chocolate,
cake cooking in the oven.
Yum!

Strawberries smell good and they taste good.

In your mouth is your tongue.

On your tongue, there are lots of small spots.

These are our *taste buds*. Taste buds taste our food.

There are sweet tastes: ice-cream, cake, chocolate.

There are salt tastes: salt, crisps.

And there are bitter tastes: lemons.
What tastes do you like?

We can feel cold things and hot things.
You have skin on your body.
Your skin touches things and you feel them.

Under your skin there are your *nerves*.
Different nerves feel different things.
Some nerves feel hot, cold, wet and dry.
Some nerves feel hurt.

Touch tells us, "Don't touch the cooker! It's hot."

Grandad said, "What *senses* are you using now, Stan?"

Stan said, "I'm *smelling* and *tasting* my ice cream. I'm *feeling* the hot sun and the sand. I'm *seeing* my friends in the sea and I'm *hearing* my friends. They're saying, 'Stan! Come and swim.'"

Grandad smiled. He said, "Go and swim with your friends, Stan."

Stan said, "Thanks, Grandad."

Picture dictionary

Listen and repeat

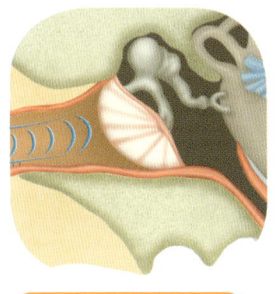
eardrum

light

loud

nerve

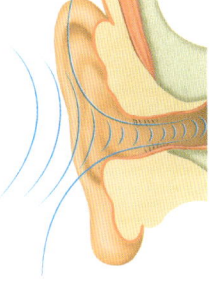
sound waves

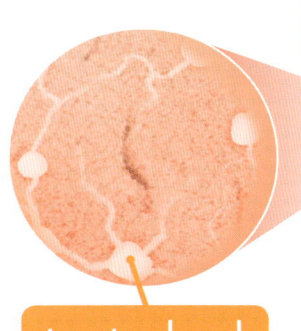
taste bud

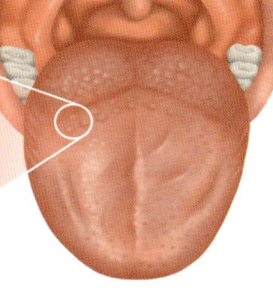
tongue

torch

After reading

1 Look and match

smell　　taste　　hear　　feel　　see

2 Listen and say

Collins

Published by Collins
An imprint of HarperCollins*Publishers*
Westerhill Road
Bishopbriggs
Glasgow
G64 2QT

HarperCollins*Publishers*
1st Floor, Watermarque Building
Ringsend Road
Dublin 4
Ireland

William Collins' dream of knowledge for all began with the publication of his first book in 1819.

A self-educated mill worker, he not only enriched millions of lives, but also founded a flourishing publishing house. Today, staying true to this spirit, Collins books are packed with inspiration, innovation and practical expertise. They place you at the centre of a world of possibility and give you exactly what you need to explore it.

© HarperCollins*Publishers* Limited 2020

10 9 8 7 6 5 4 3 2

ISBN 978-0-00-839795-1

Collins® and COBUILD® are registered trademarks of HarperCollins*Publishers* Limited

www.collins.co.uk/elt

All rights reserved. No part of this publication may be reproduced, stored in a retrieval system, or transmitted in any form by any means, electronic, mechanical, photocopying, recording or otherwise, without the prior written permission of the Publisher or a licence permitting restricted copying in the United Kingdom issued by the Copyright Licensing Agency Ltd, 5th Floor, Shackleton House, 4 Battle Bridge Lane, London SE1 2HX.

British Library Cataloguing in Publication Data

A catalogue record for this publication is available from the British Library.

All rights reserved. No part of this book may be reproduced, stored in a retrieval system, or transmitted in any form or by any means, electronic, mechanical, photocopying, recording or otherwise, without the prior permission in writing of the Publisher. This book is sold subject to the conditions that it shall not, by way of trade or otherwise, be lent, re-sold, hired out or otherwise circulated without the Publisher's prior consent in any form of binding or cover other than that in which it is published and without a similar condition including this condition being imposed on the subsequent purchaser.

Author: Anna Cowper
Illustrator: Ángeles Peinador (Beehive)
Series editor: Rebecca Adlard
Publishing manager: Lisa Todd
Product managers: Jennifer Hall and Caroline Green
In-house editor: Alma Puts Keren
Project manager: Emily Hooton
Editor: Frances Amrani
Proofreaders: Natalie Murray and Michael Lamb
Cover designer: Kevin Robbins
Typesetter: 2Hoots Publishing Services Ltd
Audio produced by id audio, London
Reading guide author: Emma Wilkinson
Production controller: Rachel Weaver
Printed and bound by: GPS Group, Slovenia

MIX
Paper from
responsible sources
FSC™ C007454

This book is produced from independently certified FSC™ paper to ensure responsible forest management.

For more information visit: www.harpercollins.co.uk/green

Download the audio for this book and a reading guide for parents and teachers at www.collins.co.uk/839795